On the Trail of the Playground Thief

Story by Carmel Reilly
Illustrations by Maria Lia Malandrino

Contents

Chapter 1

Who Took Salim's Bike?

It was Monday, and I was meeting my friend Salim before school.

Salim is always cheerful, so when I saw his glum face that morning, I knew something was wrong.

"Nina!" he wailed. "My bike has been stolen. I left it at the bike shelter on Saturday afternoon after football practice because Alex's mum gave me a lift home. When I went to check on it this morning, it was gone!"

"Oh, no! Are you sure someone didn't just move it?" I asked.

"The security cable was cut," he replied. "I've looked all over the playground, but my bike is definitely not here." He shook his head. "I don't know why anyone would want it. It's so ancient!"

We went to the office to report Salim's missing bike. It was busy that morning. We had to wait in line behind several people.

It was almost our turn when a delivery man with a trolley full of boxes came through the front door.

The office manager, Ms Morsha, waved to him and handed him some keys.

"Just pop those in the storeroom, thanks," she said, before turning to pick up the ringing phone.

When we finally got to speak to Ms Morsha, she looked concerned by our news.

"That's terrible, Salim," she said. "We'll report the theft to the police online, and you can ask your parents to do that as well when you get home later. In the meantime, I'll put out an alert on the school website and notify the staff to keep a lookout for your bike. Fingers crossed!"

"Thanks!" we said.

That afternoon, after school, Salim came over to my place.

Luckily for me, I live directly opposite school, which means it's easy for friends to come over after classes finish.

Salim rang his mum to tell her what had happened. She said she would fill out a police report online about the bike straight away. Dad made us afternoon tea.

"I'm sorry about your bike, Salim," he said. "There's an old bike in our garage you can use. I just need to oil it and pump up the tyres. I can do that now if you want to ride it home."

"That would be fantastic!" said Salim. "Thanks so much."

"And if your bike doesn't turn up, you can keep that one," said Dad. "We don't use it any more."

"I'll take good care of it!" said Salim.

Chapter 2

Another Disappearance

Salim looked much happier the next morning. "It was so good to be able to ride to school again," he said. "Plus, it's Tuesday!"

Salim and I loved Tuesdays.

On Tuesday mornings, our class helped out in the school garden, which was a large, wild space at the back of the playground.

Not only was gardening fun, but my older sister, Gabby, was the school gardener.

Gabby was grown up, and didn't live at home any more. I loved being able to see her when she came to work at school.

When we arrived that day, Gabby told us that we would be planting tomatoes. She had tubs of seedlings ready for us on a bench.

As I went to get my seedling, I noticed Gabby looking inside the gardening shed.

"Did you lose something?" I asked.

"I can't find my favourite shovel. And a wooden box, a couple of sacks and some garden stakes seem to be missing as well," Gabby replied.

"Salim's bike was stolen from the bike shelter on the weekend," I said.

"That's awful, Salim," said Gabby, frowning. "I don't know if my things were stolen, though. The shed was still locked this morning. I think I must have forgotten to put them away last Friday. I'm sure they're here somewhere. Besides, who would want old gardening things?"

"That's what I said about my old bike," said Salim. "But someone wanted it enough to cut its security cable."

Chapter 3
A Bad Night's Sleep

That night, Gabby came over to our place for dinner and told Dad about her missing gardening equipment.

"I searched all over the garden, but the shovel, box, sacks and stakes have completely disappeared," she said. "I think you were right about them being stolen, Nina. I noticed some shrubs had been dug up and taken, too!"

"Why would anyone do that?" Dad asked.

Gabby shrugged. "I suppose the thief wanted them for their own garden," she said glumly.

"It's been a busy time for thieves," said Dad. "I read in the news that there have been two jewellery shop robberies in town in the past two days."

"Two robberies?" I asked.

"Yes, they think the same thief struck twice," said Dad.

It took me a long time to get to sleep that night.

When I did, I had a scary dream that I was trying to run away from the police while carrying stolen jewels.

I woke up suddenly, my heart racing inside my chest.

It was very dark. The clock by my bed said that it was 3 am.

As I lay in the darkness, trying to get back to sleep, I thought I saw a flash of light through a gap in the curtains.

I got out of bed, carefully pushed the curtain aside and looked across the road.

I could see the dim outline of the school buildings and, further away, the bike shelter and the garden.

Everything seemed still and quiet, and I was about to go back to bed when I noticed something odd.

Someone was moving around the school garden with a flashlight!

"Dad! Dad!" I called, as I raced into his bedroom.

Dad clicked his lamp on and half sat up. His eyes were huge. "What's happened?"

"Someone's in the school garden!" I cried.

"What?" He blinked several times.

"Yes, come and see," I said. "There's a light moving around."

Dad got out of bed with a groan, and we went down the dark hallway back to my room.

We crouched next to the window and stared out into the darkness.

Nothing moved, and there were no lights to be seen.

After a while, I said, "I'm certain there was someone there."

"It was probably just a dream," said Dad, in a tired voice. "Hop back into bed. You'll be exhausted in the morning."

Chapter 4
The Locked Gate

In the morning, I was surprised that I didn't feel tired at all. I ate breakfast quickly and raced over to school.

I met Salim at the bike shelter and told him about what I had seen the night before.

"Dad said it must have been a dream, but I don't think so."

We walked over to the garden. Gabby was already there, weeding one of the garden beds.

"Did anything else go missing last night?" I asked.

Gabby shook her head. "No," she said. "Why?"

"I saw someone with a flashlight here last night," I said.

"All my tools are here, including the new shovel I bought yesterday," said Gabby. "Although I haven't had a good look around. We can check together."

The three of us inspected the garden.

"Oh, no," said Gabby, as we came to one of the garden beds near the back fence. "Some more of these shrubs have been taken."

Looking at the bed, I realised there was a trail of dirt leading away from it towards the back gate.

"It looks like the thief went out there!" I said.

Gabby looked puzzled. "That gate is always locked," she said. "I have a key in the shed. I'll go and get it so we can see if there are any traces of dirt outside."

But, just then, the bell rang.

"We'll have to come back after school," I called, as Salim and I raced off to class.

Chapter 5

On the Trail

When we went back to the garden after school, Gabby had unlocked the back gate.

"Look. You can see the trail of dirt," she said, pointing up the path.

"Shall we investigate?" I asked.

"I just need to let Mum know I'm going to be home a bit late," said Salim.

Gabby phoned Salim's mum. Then she grinned. "All right, let's see where this trail goes."

We followed the dirt trail for a few minutes, until we reached a small park.

"It seems to stop here," said Salim, staring at the ground.

We were standing there, uncertain about what to do next, when a man came out of a house across the road. He walked towards a bike.

"Look at those orange stickers on the bike, Salim," I said, as we watched the man walk the bike through the gate. "Isn't that –"

"My bike!" Salim gasped.

“We need to call the police,” said Gabby, as the bike and its rider sped along the road and disappeared around the corner.

We walked closer so Gabby could see the number of the house to tell the police.

The place was very old, with an overgrown garden, but we could tell immediately that one small part of it had been tidied up.

“Are those your plants over there?” Salim asked, as we stared across the fence.

“I think they are!” said Gabby. “They still have the tags on them from the nursery where I bought them. And those are the stolen stakes being used to hold them up. And that’s my shovel on the ground, too!”

When Gabby got through to the police, they told her that they would arrive soon.

We went across to the park to wait for them.

It wasn't long before the man with the bike returned to the house.

"He looks familiar," said Salim, as we watched the man get off his bike. "I've seen him somewhere before."

The man had just gone inside when a police car arrived. Gabby waved to the police and we walked over.

"You got here quickly," Gabby said. "We haven't been waiting long."

"We were already on our way here," said one of the police officers, who introduced herself as Officer Su. "The person who lives here is a suspect in some jewellery shop robberies, and we were coming to interview him."

Gabby pointed to the plants in the front garden. "Well," she said sternly, "he also stole a bike, as well as those plants and that shovel from our school garden!"

Chapter 6

Digging Down

We waited while the police officers went into the house.

A little while later, Officer Su came back outside. "The suspect claims he's innocent," she said. "And, what's more, we've searched all over the house, and we can't find any signs of the jewellery anywhere."

"At least you can arrest him for stealing our gardening things and my bike," said Salim.

As Salim spoke, I suddenly realised why the thief had taken our things.

"That's it!" I exclaimed. "He's buried the jewellery in the garden! He stole the shrubs so he could cover up the spot."

Officer Su raised her eyebrows. "Let's test your theory."

She stepped across the front garden, picked up Gabby's shovel and carefully started to dig up the newly planted shrubs.

After a moment, she shouted, "Look at this!" Officer Su pulled a gardening sack out of the ground.

When she opened the sack up, we saw it held smaller bags, each one filled with rings, necklaces and watches.

Later, Officer Su told us that the thief had a part-time job delivering supplies to our school.

"Of course!" said Salim. "That's where I recognised his face from. He was in the office on Monday, dropping off boxes."

At some stage, the thief had stolen an extra set of keys from the office, which gave him access to the school gates and the garden shed. When the time was right, he stole Salim's bike to use as a getaway vehicle in the robbery. Then he took the garden equipment and plants so that he could bury the stolen goods. Anyone looking at his house would just think that he'd been doing some gardening.

"The thief thought the police might suspect him and search his house," said Officer Su. "But he was sure no one would think to search his garden. If you three hadn't gone looking for your things, we may have never found those jewels. Well done!"

The next day at school, Salim and I were famous. Everyone knew about how we had helped to track down the stolen goods.

The principal, Mr Meadows, even mentioned us at assembly. "Nina and Salim are our top detectives," he said.

Salim looked at me. We had been talking since the night before about starting a detective agency, but we couldn't think of a name.

"That's it!" he said. "Top Detectives."

"Top Detectives," I echoed. "And we're ready to solve the next mystery!"